Happy C

THE LITTLEST
PIRATE
IN A PICKLE

NICHOLAS NOSH IS TEASED
BY HIS COUSIN PRIMROSE FOR
BEING SO SMALL. BUT WHEN
CAPTAIN MANNERS OF THE JOLLY
DODGER KIDNAPS HER, NICHOLAS
SHOWS JUST HOW BRAVE A

LITTL

Happy Cat First Readers

THE LITTLEST PIRATE
IN A PICKLE

SHERRYL
CLARK

ILLUSTRATED BY
TOM JELLETT

HAPPY CAT BOOKS

Published by
Happy Cat Books
An imprint of Catnip Publishing Ltd
14 Greville Street
London EC1N 8SB

First published by Penguin Books, Australia, 2007

This edition first published 2007
1 3 5 7 9 10 8 6 4 2

Text copyright © Sherryl Clark, 2007
Illustrations copyright © Tom Jellet, 2007

The moral rights of the author and illustrator have been asserted

A CIP catalogue record for this book is available
from the British Library

ISBN: 978-1-905117-56-7

Printed in Poland

www.catnippublishing.co.uk

For Mia. *S.C.*

For Jack. *T.J.*

Chapter One

Nicholas Nosh, the littlest pirate in the world, woke up early. He was too excited to sleep. Today he was taking part in the Pirate Games. He'd been practising for weeks with his cannonballs.

He got dressed and ran downstairs.

'We're waiting for your aunt and uncle,' said his mum. 'This is their first visit in ten years.'

Nicholas heard a noise like someone blowing a rusty tin horn, and then the doorbell rang.

He opened the door. There stood Uncle Wartle, Aunt Peanuckle and a little girl. The girl had curly brown hair, and she wore a pretty pink dress and pink shoes.

'Hello,' she hooted. 'You must be my cousin. I'm Primrose. You're not very big, are you?'

How rude! Nicholas thought. And her voice would frighten cows!

He kissed Aunt Peanuckle and shook Uncle

Wartle's hand. His uncle
peered at him from under
bushy black eyebrows and
said, 'Hmph.'

'Are you going to the Games?' Primrose bellowed. 'What events are you in? Are you any good?'

Nicholas shuddered.

It was going to be a very long day.

Chapter Two

The Pirate Games were
held every year. There were
events like Heaving the
Cannonball, Tossing the
Pike, Cutlass Duelling and
Axe Throwing. The prizes
were large gold cups.

'I suppose you're too

short to enter most events,'
Primrose said. 'They'd be
worried you'd get hurt.'

'I'm not short,' Nicholas said.

'Yes, you are.'

The bell rang for Heaving the Cannonball to start.

Nicholas chose a nice round cannonball.

Ready, steady, go!

He skipped forward and heaved the cannonball as far as he could.

It was an excellent throw, and everybody clapped.

Eight much bigger
pirates took part in the
event, but Nicholas won!

That night, at dinner, Nicholas showed everyone his big shiny cup. Uncle Wartle inspected it to make sure it was real gold.

Primrose stuffed a piece of plum pie into her mouth. 'One gold cup is nothing,' she said. 'That's not being a real pirate. Real pirates sail the high seas and steal treasure.'

Primrose's voice ground

into Nicholas's head.
He stuck his fingers in
his ears, but he could still
hear her.

'Listen!' he snapped.
'I have a ship. I have
treasure. I am a real
pirate.'

'No way,' she said. 'You're
just too short.'

Nicholas's face turned
bright red. 'Fine,' he said.
'Tomorrow we'll go out
on my ship the *Golden
Pudding* and attack
somebody and steal their
treasure. All right?'

Primrose stuffed another piece of plum pie into her mouth. 'Sounds like fun,' she said.

Chapter Three

In the morning Nicholas
wished he'd kept his mouth
shut. As his pirate crew got
the *Golden Pudding* ready
to sail, Gretta, who was
chief cook and first mate,
joined him on the deck.

'I don't want to attack

anybody,' Nicholas said.
'We've never done anything
like that before. We've only
rescued people.'

'Don't worry,' Gretta said. 'Everybody is still at the Pirate Games. No one will be out today.'

'Here I am,' Primrose said, bounding up the gangplank. Today she wore a sparkly blue dress and white shoes. Nothing like proper pirate gear.

'Let's go then,' Nicholas said crossly.

The *Golden Pudding*

edged out of the harbour.

'Where are we going?'
Primrose said. 'Have you
got a map? Are there
any islands with buried
treasure? Have you got lots
of cannonballs?'

'One the size of your
mouth would be good,'
Gretta grumbled under her
breath as she went below to
cook lunch.

Nicholas was left on deck

with Primrose. She talked
non-stop. The other pirates
stuck their fingers in
their ears.

They sailed all morning
in search of a ship, but the
wide blue sea was empty.

'Let's go home,' Nicholas
said at last.

'Wait,' Primrose said.
'I can see a ship.'

Nicholas looked through
his spyglass. Yes, it was

a ship, but it looked old and shabby. There were holes in its sails.

'Let's attack!' Primrose said, hopping up and down the deck like a demented frog.

'I don't think that's a good idea,' Nicholas said. 'It doesn't look like a treasure ship.'

'Are you a chicken?' Primrose asked. 'Short

people often are afraid.'

'I'm not scared!' Nicholas

shouted. 'And I'm not
short!'

Chapter Four

Nicholas ordered his crew
to get the cannons ready
for firing.

Gretta came up on deck,
carrying a tray of meat
pies. Primrose ate three.
'Do your pirates know what
to do?' she asked.

'Of course,' Nicholas said.

But he wasn't sure *he* knew

what to do.

How did you attack

another ship? Did you fire
a warning shot first?

He used his spyglass
again. Now they were
closer, he could see the
name *Jolly Dodger* painted
on the ship's stern. The
paint was peeling and
the anchor was rusty.
Two grubby sailors sat on
covered boxes stacked on
the deck.

'Don't let them get away,'

said Primrose. She ran
to the bow and shouted,
'Avast, me hearties. Yo ho
ho and a bottle of rum!'

Gretta raised her
eyebrows. 'She's read too
many pirate books.'

Nicholas sighed. 'Let's
get this over with. Fire
a cannon!'

Boom! The cannonball
sailed through the air and
landed with a big splash

in front of the other ship.

'Surrender, you dogs!'

Primrose shouted, waving

her arms. 'Show the white flag!'

Suddenly everything changed. As Nicholas watched, lots of pirates rushed up from below the *Jolly Dodger*'s decks.

They pulled the covers off the boxes to reveal a row of cannons.

Boom! Boom!
Cannonballs flew around the *Golden Pudding*. One

landed on the foredeck,

making a big hole. Bits of

wood flew everywhere.

Primrose was knocked

over. Gretta helped her up
and brushed her down. She
was unhurt, but at least
she'd stopped talking.

Nicholas, standing at the
ship's wheel, was frozen
with shock.

Chapter Five

A man dressed all in black stood at the rail of the *Jolly Dodger*. He said, 'Actually, I want *you* to surrender, if you wouldn't mind, thank you very much.'

Nicholas looked at Gretta. 'Do I have to?' he asked.

'I'm afraid so,' she said.
'He has a bigger crew and
more cannons. But he's
very polite.'

Nicholas and his crew
piled all their cutlasses in
the middle of the deck.

The captain of the *Jolly*

Dodger stepped on board the *Golden Pudding* and bowed. His oily black hair shone in the sun.

'Pleased to meet you, young sir,' he said. 'I am Captain Manners. Hand over your treasure.'

'Er . . . we don't have any,' Nicholas said.

'Are you not real pirates?' asked Captain Manners.

'Yes, but . . .'

'What are you doing on our ship?' Primrose said in her foghorn voice. 'Go away, you nasty man. And take your scabby crew with you.'

Captain Manners peered down at her. 'And who are you, little girl?' he said.

Primrose put her hands on her hips. 'I'm Primrose Crimpet.'

'Any relation to the rich banker Wartle Crimpet?'

Captain Manners asked.

'He's my father,' Primrose said. 'He could buy your ship and turn it into firewood in two minutes.'

'I'm sure he could,' Captain Manners said. 'And he could also afford a very large ransom.'

With that, he put Primrose under his arm and leaped over the rail to the *Jolly Dodger*. He waved

at Nicholas. 'Tell Wartle Crimpet it will cost him ten chests filled with gold pieces to get his daughter back,' he shouted.

Chapter Six

The *Jolly Dodger* sailed
away. Primrose was tied to
the mainmast, a gag over
her mouth.

The *Golden Pudding*
seemed so peaceful now.
But when Nicholas thought
of sailing home and telling

Uncle Wartle that Primrose had been kidnapped, he felt all cold and sweaty.

'You've got yourself in a real pickle,' Gretta said. 'We'd better get help.'

'No way,' Nicholas said. 'I have to rescue her myself.'

'How?' asked Gretta.

'I don't know,' Nicholas said. 'Let's follow them, and I'll try to come up with a plan.'

The *Golden Pudding* set
sail, following the *Jolly
Dodger* at a distance.

Nicholas kept watch with

his spyglass. Every time the pirates took Primrose's gag off to feed her, he could hear her voice hooting across the water.

After a whole week Gretta said, 'Nicholas, we have no food left. Not even anything to catch fish with. We have to go home.'

Nicholas imagined Uncle Wartle's angry face. 'Just one more day. Please.'

'All right,' Gretta said grumpily. *'One.'*

Late that afternoon the *Jolly Dodger* dropped anchor by an island, and the pirates went ashore. Soon it was dark. Nicholas couldn't see if any of the crew were left on board.

'It's now or never,' he said to Gretta.

Together they lowered the ship's boat.

Trying not to make any
noise, Nicholas rowed
across to the *Jolly Dodger*,
and climbed the ladder.

Chapter Seven

In a few seconds Nicholas
was on board the *Jolly
Dodger*. There were no
lamps on, and he could
barely see a thing.

As he crept forward,
feeling his way around,
his hand landed on

something bristly. Was it

a pirate's beard?

He stopped, his heart pounding.

Rroowwwllllllll! Hissssss! The bristly thing was the mangy ship's cat!

Nicholas edged forward again. Sweat trickled down his neck.

His finger connected with someone's eye.

'Mmmmfffrrrghh!'

Nicholas felt around the person's head.

Curly hair, mouth gag. It
was Primrose.

He untied her, not

stopping to take the gag off. They scrambled down the ladder and into the boat, and then Nicholas rowed back to the *Golden Pudding*.

Back on board, in the lamplight, Nicholas saw that there was a note pinned on Primrose's dress.

TAKE HER - PLEASE!!!

He tried very hard not to laugh, but he couldn't stop himself.

Then Primrose saw the note. Big tears rolled down her face.

Nicholas stopped laughing and untied the gag. 'Sorry,' he said.

'I just want to be a pirate!' sobbed Primrose. 'Mummy and Daddy make me wear these stupid girly

dresses and learn stupid
things like embroidery.'
Her sobs grew louder.

'Please be quiet,' Nicholas

said. 'I'll teach you how to
be a pirate.'

Primrose stopped crying.
'You will?'

'I'll even lend you my pirate hat,' Nicholas said. 'But only if you promise to stop saying I'm short.'

'Yo ho ho!' Primrose grabbed a cutlass and waved it around, nearly taking off a pirate's arm. 'Arrrr, arrrrr!' she cried.

Nicholas sighed.

It was going to be a long trip home.

From Sherryl Clark

I love writing stories about
Nicholas – I think it's very
fitting that the 'littlest pirate'
is always the one who has to
rescue other people. But one
day I might have to write a
story where Nicholas captures
lots of treasure, all on his own.
He deserves it!

From Tom Jellett

It's always good to find out
what Nicholas Nosh is up to
and to see how he's grown.
Actually, he hasn't grown very
much at all, but that's just
fine, as I quite like him being
short. It's fun to draw him with
a very big hat and standing
on a small box just to see over
the *Golden Pudding*'s helm.
('Helm' is a fancy boaty word
for 'steering-wheel'.)

Nicholas Nosh is the littlest pirate in the world. He's not allowed
to go to sea. 'You're too small,' said his dad. But when the fierce
pirate Captain Red Beard kidnaps his family, Nicholas sets sail
to rescue them!

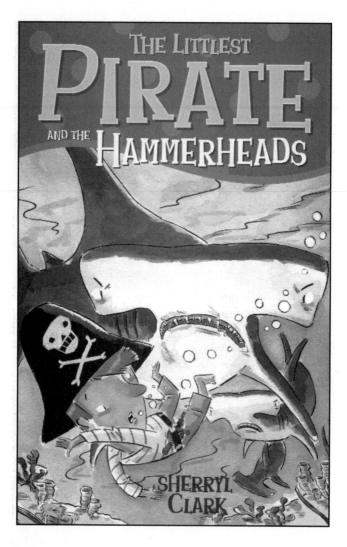

Nicholas Nosh, the littlest pirate in the world, has to rescue his family's treasure which has been stolen by Captain Hammerhead. But how can he outwit the sharks that are guarding Captain Hammerhead's ship?

Jock can make a special sound like a duck!
If you can learn to make it too you can help Jock rescue the
little duck from the duck hunter. Quick, before it's too late!

David's had a party invitation!
It's a dressing-up party and he's going to go as a fox. But
when he arrives he can see he's made a mistake in choosing
his costume. Can he still fit in with the party theme and
have fun?

The Gorilla Suit

Victor Kelleher

Tom was given a gorilla suit for his birthday. He loved it and wore it everywhere. When mum and dad took him to the zoo he wouldn't wear his ordinary clothes. But isn't it asking for trouble to go to the zoo dressed as a gorilla?

First day at new school for Kerry.
It's easy to get lost in a big new school when you don't
know anyone. But a helpful dog shows Kerry the way to the
playground - and to lots of new friends!

Nobody is better at being bad than Buster Reed – he flicks
paint, says rude words to girls, sticks chewing gum under
the seats and wears the same socks for weeks at a time.
Naturally no one wants to know him. But Buster has a
secret – he would like a friend to play with.
How will he ever manage to find one?

The Princess and the Unicorn

Wendy Blaxland

No one believes in unicorns any more. Except Princess Lily, that is.
So when the king falls ill and the only thing that can cure him is
the magic of a unicorn, it's up to her to find one.
But can Lily find a magical unicorn in time?